YOSHIKO
AND THE
FOREIGNER

MIMI OTEY LITTLE

Frances Foster Books • Farrar, Straus and Giroux • New York

To a good Japanese girl who spoke to a foreigner

Copyright © 1996 by Mimi Otey Little

All rights reserved. Published simultaneously in Canada by HarperCollins*CanadaLtd.* Printed in the United States of America by
Berryville Graphics. Color separations by Hong Kong Scanner Arts. Typography by Filomena Tuosto. First edition, 1996

Library of Congress Cataloging-in-Publication Data
Little, Mimi Otey.
Yoshiko and the foreigner / Mimi Otey Little. — 1st ed.
p.   cm.   Frances Foster Books   [1. Prejudices—Fiction.   2. Japan—Fiction.   3. Interracial marriage—Fiction.]
I. Title.   PZ7.L723Yo   1996   95-33512   CIP   AC

"Attention, all passengers. We regret to inform you that this will be the last stop for this train. To continue to Tokyo, please take the train across the platform. We are sorry for the inconvenience."

Yoshiko groaned. It was hot. The train was crowded. And now it had broken down.

One man stayed on the broken-down train. A gaijin, Yoshiko thought. A foreigner. He didn't understand the announcement. Too bad—I'd like to help him. But good Japanese girls don't talk to foreigners. Especially Americans wearing military uniform. Yoshiko sighed.

The conductor came gesturing and spouting words. The young Air Force officer broke into a big sheepish grin. "Thank you, conductor, sir!" He jumped up and crossed the platform. Yoshiko watched curiously through the window. Such a warm smile. He doesn't act like a gaijin. In fact, he seems almost nice.

But when the young officer caught her eye above the heads of their fellow passengers, her cheeks flushed. Why do I have to be so tall, she thought. The American fumbled for his Japanese phrase book and cleared his throat. "I beg your pardon, but the road has disappeared," he said loudly in Japanese.

The passengers tittered quietly with amusement. I will ignore him, Yoshiko said to herself. Maybe he will ask someone else.

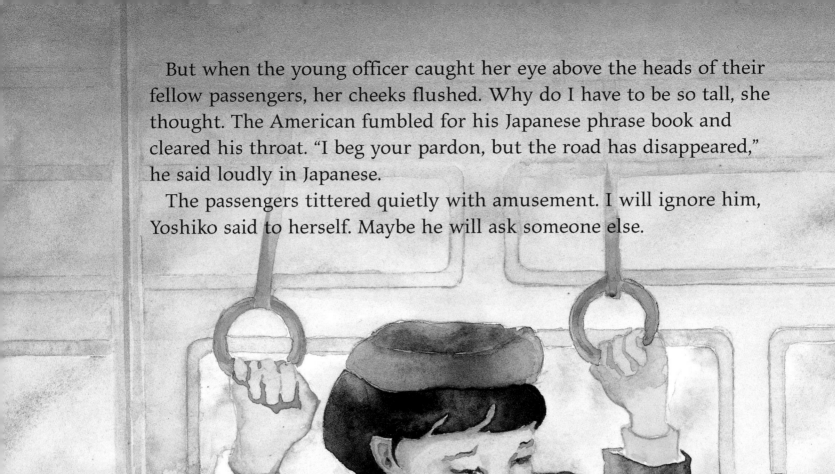

But the young officer tried again. "I am a dancing girl. Where is the doctor?" The whole car erupted into giggles.

Why must he speak to me, Yoshiko thought. Doesn't he know not to talk to good Japanese girls?

But he didn't, and he tried again. "You see, I am a boiled pepper."

The car roared with laughter. Yoshiko smiled. It is hot, she thought. He is lost. I don't care what people think! "Sir," she said in perfect English, "can I help you?"

The American wanted to see the Emperor's palace. So Yoshiko told him how to get there.

"Would you like to go with me?" he asked when they reached Tokyo.

Yoshiko answered carefully. "I will have to ask my sister. If she says yes, I will meet you at the entrance gates of the palace."

Yoshiko's eldest sister, Kazuko, lived in the city. "Who is he?" she asked.

"Just a fellow who was lost on the train."

"And you helped him?" Kazuko asked.

"Yes." Yoshiko paused. "He came from the countryside," she added, careful to omit that he was a foreigner.

"Well, just get home by dinnertime," said her sister.

When Yoshiko got home, she did not mention the American. Nor did she mention him when she saw him again a week later. And again. And again.

Not to her sisters or brothers. Not to her mother. Not to her aunts or uncles. Not to any of her cousins or even to her little nephew. And especially not to her father.

The young officer, whose name was Flem, soon began to ask, "Have you mentioned me to your family?"

She would answer, "It's not time yet."

So Flem contented himself with asking questions.

"What is your house like?"

"Well, it's big," said Yoshiko, "and there is a garden. In the garden there is a fish-pond. My father used to raise the most beautiful fish. But now he is old and the fish have long since died."

The next time they met in the city, Flem was holding a glass bowl. In the bowl were two beautiful fish.

"I raised them myself," he said. "I'd like your father to have them."

It was late summer. "Tell me more about your home in the countryside," he asked again.

"Well, in the main room we have a miniature shrine for our ancestors. We fill the bowls with wine and rice. It is as if we are giving a feast for our ancestors. We use fresh boiled rice, and fine rice wine. This is how we pay our respects."

The next week, Flem gave Yoshiko two small packages.
"What are they?" she asked.
"The finest rice and wine I could find," he answered.
"They are for your family. I want to pay my
respects, too."

Months came and went. Flem continued
to court Yoshiko. But one day he received
orders to return to the United
States. So he promised to
write, and he left Japan.

A week passed.
Then two weeks.
Yoshiko heard nothing.

A month later, a letter arrived. She did not open it until she was on the train to Tokyo. Inside the first letter was another, addressed to her father. Yoshiko's stop came, but she did not get off. Instead, she stayed on the train and rode for hours. She was thinking. The letter had read simply, "Will you come to America? Will you be my wife?"

That evening Yoshiko sat with her mother and father, two sisters
and three brothers, two aunts and two uncles, seven cousins, two
nieces and one nephew, eating dinner. "I have met someone special,"
she said quietly. Everyone stopped eating. She pulled a photograph
from the folds of her kimono. "This is he."

There were gasps and everyone spoke at once. "What is this? This is a gaijin! He is a soldier! An American soldier! You've been seeing an American soldier! Yoshiko! What are you thinking? Papa, say something!"

But Yoshiko's father was silent. His face was grave. "Eat," he said after several moments. "The food will get cold."

When Mr. Sasagawa finished eating, he rose and moved to the ancestral altar in the corner of the big room. "Yoshiko-chan." Yoshiko quickly rose and joined her father in front of the shrine. All the rest of Yoshiko's family came, too.

Taking fresh rice from a lacquered box and a bottle of fine plum wine, Mr. Sasagawa refilled the sacred bowls. "This American, he will not understand the ways of our people. Americans only laugh and scoff at our customs."

"Forgive my interruption, Father, but this rice and plum wine were gifts from the American," Yoshiko said. "When I told him about our family shrine, he wanted to see it. Even when I told him he would not be welcome, he still wanted to pay his respects."

Mr. Sasagawa turned and went out into the garden.
"Yoshiko-chan!" Yoshiko went, too. The family followed.
"Americans are fast people," he said. "They are complicated;
they think highly of their own advancement."

"Yes, Father, but these fish, they belonged to the American. He raised them. I told him about your fishpond, Father. He wanted you to have them."

Mr. Sasagawa returned to the dinner table. Yoshiko waited. The family waited. "Yoshiko-chan!" Yoshiko came. And, of course, the family came.

"America is full of proud people. This American could not understand what it means to honor our family and our people."

"Father, Mother, forgive me again. The American does understand. He has honored us. He has even learned to speak our language."

Now Yoshiko took the letter from the fold of her kimono. On the envelope, "Most Honorable Sasagawa-san" was written in perfect Japanese characters. "He has also learned to write it." Yoshiko laid the letter on the table in front of her father.

One by one, the family slipped out of the room. Finally, Yoshiko left, too. Her mother and father sat staring at the letter.

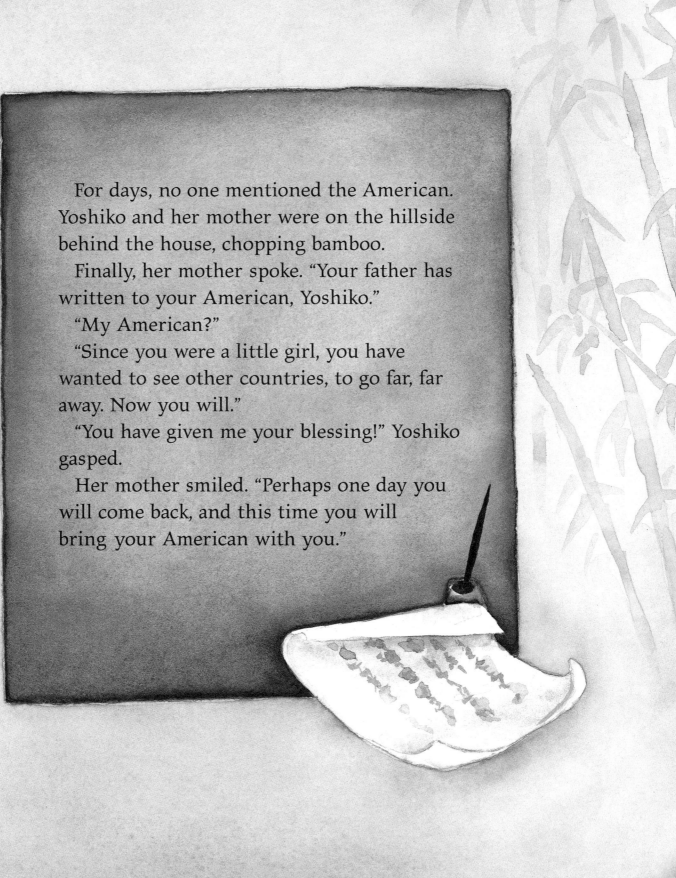

For days, no one mentioned the American. Yoshiko and her mother were on the hillside behind the house, chopping bamboo.

Finally, her mother spoke. "Your father has written to your American, Yoshiko."

"My American?"

"Since you were a little girl, you have wanted to see other countries, to go far, far away. Now you will."

"You have given me your blessing!" Yoshiko gasped.

Her mother smiled. "Perhaps one day you will come back, and this time you will bring your American with you."

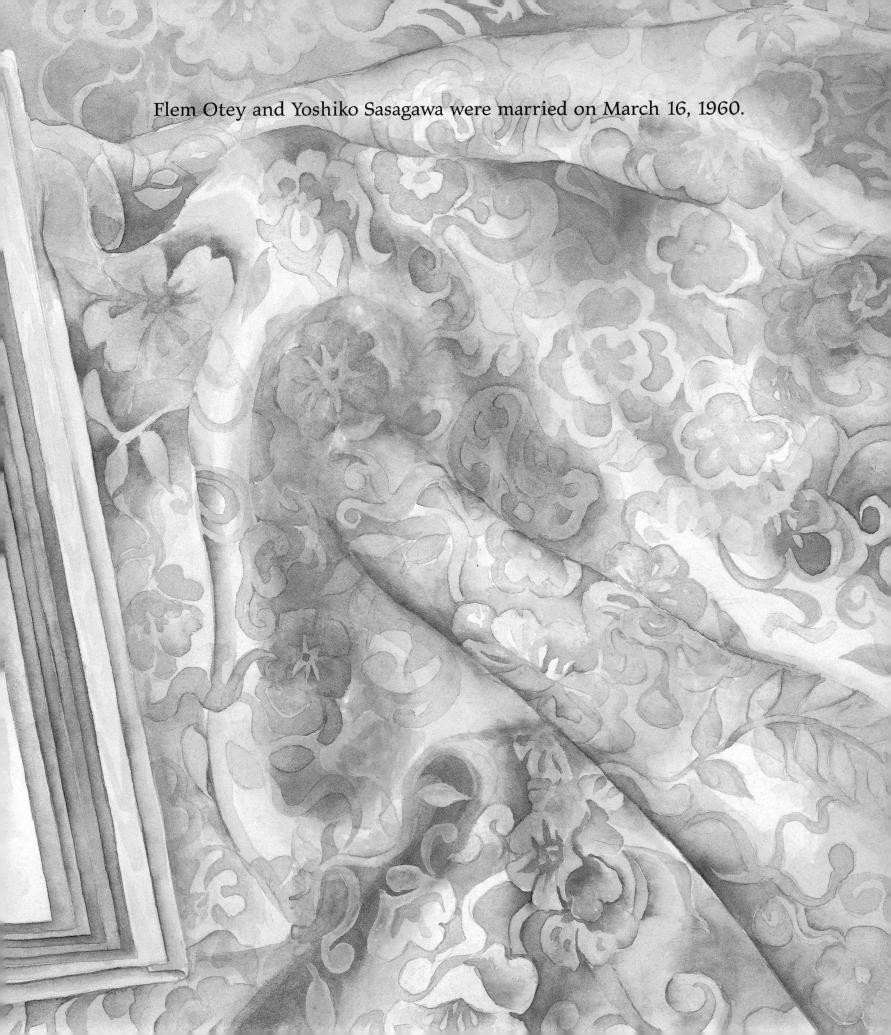

Flem Otey and Yoshiko Sasagawa were married on March 16, 1960.